엘리트 시선 36

살구꽃 피는 마을

장 현 경 시집

엘리트출판사

이 도서의 국립중앙도서관 출판예정도서목록(CIP)은
서지정보유통지원시스템 홈페이지(http://seoji.nl.go.kr)와
국가자료종합목록 구축시스템(http://kolis-net.nl.go.kr)에서 이용하실 수 있습니다.
(CIP제어번호 : CIP2020035064)

살구꽃 피는 마을

장 현 경 시집

엘리트출판사

아름다운 꽃들의 이야기

처서를 지나면 곧 가을이 온다. 독서의 계절이다. 송나라의 태종이 1천 권의 책을 1년에 읽었다고 하자, 이에 신하들이 건강을 염려하니, 책을 펼치기만 해도 유익하므로 괜찮다고 말했는데 이로 인해 '개권유익(開券有益)'이라는 명언이 탄생했다. 오나라의 손권은 '수불석권(手不釋券)'이라는 고사성어를 이용하여 아무리 바빠도 책을 손에서 놓지 말라고 측근들에게 타일렀다.

위나라의 현자(賢者), 동우는 '삼여(三餘)의 교훈' 즉 1년의 나머지는 겨울이요, 하루의 나머지는 밤이며, 농사철의 나머지는 비올 때이니, 그때 책을 읽으면 된다고 하였다. 좋은 시는 독자에게 감동을 주므로 오래 남는다. 시는 생명력이 있어 작가가 작고한 후에도 오래도록 남아 후세에 영향을 주고 독자의 심리적 변화를 자극한다.

삶은 유한하다. 추운 겨울이 지나가면 봄이 온다. 꽃이 피어 사람들의 마음을 즐겁게 해 준다. 부겐빌레아꽃 사랑초꽃 갯버들꽃이 아름다운 자태를 뽐내고 있다. 긴 긴 겨울을 이겨낸 꽃나무들이 계절을 초월하여 자신의 아름다움을 꽃을 피워 보여주고 있다.

　꽃을 보니 마음이 밝아지고 기분마저 좋아진다. 시인으로 움츠린 몸에 기지개를 켜며 사계절 지지 않는 꽃들의 이야기를 소재로 여기 한 권의 영역 시집을 다듬는다. 늘 따뜻한 성원을 보내주신 가족과 이웃의 지지에 고마운 마음 전하며 청계문학 가족여러분의 건승을 빕니다. 나의 시편들을 만나는 존경하는 독자님들께 건강과 행복이 늘 함께하시기를 기원합니다.

2020년 7월 청계서재(淸溪書齋)에서
자정(紫井) 장현경(張鉉景) 삼가 씀

꽃과 함께

봄과 여름 그리고 가을

대지에는 바람 소리
우 우
흐르는 물소리
졸졸 졸

억겁으로 아로새긴 꽃들이
계절로
연월일로
만나고 사랑하고

기쁘고
즐겁게
반가워하는 몸짓

세월은 흘러
펄펄 눈이 내리고

겨울꽃에서 인내를
웃음꽃에서 겸손을 배우자.

With Flowers

Spring and summer and autumn

The sound of wind on the earth
Wow
Flowing water
Solzole

The flowers that have been hanging over the years
Seasonally
By Year, by month, by day
Meet and love

With joy
Delightfully
A welcome gesture

The years pass
With a flutter of snow

Persevering in winter flowers
Humility in laughter.

contents

제1부 안개꽃과 함께

제2부 아네모네꽃

제3부 불두화의 미소

제4부 코스모스 연가

제5부 눈새기꽃

제1부

안개꽃과 함께

우리가 꿈꾸는 행복은
꽃향기와 같은 웃음
그 안에 있다

무궁화 예찬

겨레의 이상화로 추앙받는
무궁화
민족혼의 주체이며
운명공동체다

나라꽃으로 사랑받고
약용으로
활용될 수 있는 국화(國花)는
만병통치의 명약
인류에게도 행복을 주는 명화(名花)

선사 이래로
면면히 피어나는 장수화(長壽花)
끊임없이 이어지는 조국애로
민족의식을 가슴속에 수놓네!

비에 씻긴 가지
정겨운 꽃 울타리 만들고
고운 연초록 색조는
영롱한 이슬에 젖어
청아한 빛을 발하며

흘러가는 구름처럼
은은한 꽃잎은
자색의 엷은 종이인 양
뙤약볕 여름날에
활짝 피었네!

Admiration of Mugunghwa

Revered for the idealization of the nation
Mugunghwa
The subject of national spirit
A community of fate

Loved by the country flowers
For medicinal purposes
The national flower that can be used
A master of panacea
A masterpiece that gives happiness to mankind

Since the prehistoric times
Longevity flower blooming continually
A constant domestic love
You embroidered your national consciousness in your heart!

A rain-washed branch
I'm gonna make a nice flower fence
The fine green shades
In a dazzling dew
With a clear light

Like a flowing cloud
The subtle petals
A pale purple paper
On a sunny summer day
You're blooming!

개나리꽃

춘삼월 꽃샘추위에
때늦은 진눈깨비가 내렸다

먹구름 사이로 따사로운 햇살 타고
흐르는 개나리 눈망울

올망졸망
여미어 도사린 긴 잠에서 깨어

송알송알
"봄이 왔어요"
몸을 뒤척이는 소리
들리는 듯

가는 겨울에
빛의 물결
노랗게 퍼져가네!

Forsythia

A cold weather in March
The late sleet fell

In the warm sunshine through the dark clouds
A flowing forsythia eye

Olmanzol net
I wake up from a long sleep

Song al-song
"Spring is here"
A rumbling sound
As if it were audible

In the thin winter
Wave of light
It's spreading yellow!

안개꽃과 함께

우리가 꿈꾸는 행복은
꽃향기와 같은 웃음
그 안에 있다

눈이 부시게 보석같이
빛이 나는 순백의 안개꽃이 있어

사랑하는 임에게
청초한 안개꽃, 장미꽃, 백합꽃 한 다발
가슴에 꼭 안겨 드리리

그 임 오시는 그 길에
향기로운 꽃다발을 펼쳐놓고
영원히
그대를 사랑하리.

With the Gypsophila

The happiness we dream of
A smile like a flower scent
Be in there

Like a jewel with a blind eye
There's a pure white gypsophila that glows

To the beloved
A bunch of gypsophila, roses, lily flowers
I'll give you deeply in your heart

That coming is the way
The fragrant bouquet is spread
Forever
I will love you.

사랑초꽃은

봄날의 아침 해가
대지에 닿자마자
말없이 퍼진다

언제 어디에 심어도
조화롭게 피어
서로를 감싸 안는다

잡초처럼 번식하여
고요 속의 적료(寂寥)
대지가 침묵하고 있다

밤하늘의 별이 반짝일 때
꿈을 꾸고

잎이 시들어 가면서
싹을 틔우며
겨울에 꽃망울도 터트린다.

Oxalis Flower

The morning sun of spring
As soon as it reaches the earth
Spread silently

When and wherever you plant
Harmoniously blooming
Embrace each other

Breed like weeds
The loneliness in the stillness
The earth is silent

When the stars in the night sky shine
Dreaming

Withered leaves
Sprouting
Flowers burst in winter.

제라늄꽃

봄에 만난 제라늄꽃
아쉬움을 뒤로한 채
떠나려는데

꽃은 지지 않고
여름 지나 가을에도 피네

내가 그리운가
꽃이 그리워하는가

인간의 정이 천 길이라 하지만
제라늄꽃에 비할 수는 없으리

제라늄꽃
겨울에도 화분에서
'생긋 웃으며'
피어있네!

Geranium Flower

Geranium flowers we met in spring
With regret behind
I'm leaving

Without flowers
Blooming summer and autumn, too

Do you miss me?
Do you miss flowers?

I mean, human heart is a thousand lengths
Can't compare to a geranium flower

Geranium flower
In the winter, in the flowerpot
'Smiling'
It's blooming!

금낭화(錦囊花)

봄바람에
이슬비가 부슬부슬 내리고

장독대에 금낭화가
주렁주렁

담장 앞에
초롱초롱

뜰 앞에선
살랑살랑

군집을 이루어
시위를 하네!

Bleeding Heart

In the spring breeze
The drizzle is drizzling

Bleeding heart flower at jars
It's all over the place

In front of the fence
Lively

In front of the courtyard
Salang salang

In a cluster
We're protesting!

부겐빌레아꽃

에게해 섬들
인접한 정열의 나라
하얀 집
하얀 담장
하얀 부겐빌레아꽃

봄 여름 가을에 피고
베란다
화분에 심은 꽃 속의 꽃
겨울에도 피어

지상 어디에나
없는 곳이 없는
정열의 꽃

그곳에
오늘도 가 보고 싶다.

Bougenvillea Flower

Aegean islands
A country of adjoining passion
A white house
White fence
White bougenvillea flower

Blooming in spring and summer, fall
Veranda
Flowers in flowers planted in pots
In winter

Everywhere on the ground
A placeless
A flower of passion

There
I'd like to go today.

양귀비꽃

유럽이 원산지인 양귀비꽃
전쟁터에서 산화한 용사들을 기리는 꽃

전쟁 기념일마다
양귀비꽃 모양의 장식품을 옷에 달고
전쟁의 상흔을 일깨우고
잊지 않기 위해 추모한다

나라마다 시를 지어 낭송하고
묘지 둘레에
양귀비꽃을 심어 애도한다

양귀비꽃을 이미지로 만든
화폐와 기념품
붉은색이 강렬하고 더욱 돋보여
삶의 의욕이 솟는다

그림의 이미지 배경에
양귀비꽃 흐드러지게 피어
기도하는 병사의 모습에서
더욱 비장함을 느낀다

전몰자들이 누워있는 저 들녘에는
오늘도 양귀비꽃 피고 자라난다.

Poppy Flower

Poppy flowers native to Europe
Flowers to honor oxidized warriors on the battlefield

Every war anniversary
The ornament of the poppy flower shape is on the clothes
To awaken the scars of war
I remember to remember

I write poems from every country
Around the cemetery
I mourn with poppy flowers

Image-making
Money and souvenirs
Red is intense and more prominent
I am motivated by life

In the image background of the drawing
Poppy flower bloom
In the image of a soldier praying
Feel more spleen

In those fields where the war dead lie
Today, poppy flowers are growing.

상사화(相思花)

상큼하고
고결한 꽃
연 노란빛 얼굴

잎이 나올 때는
꽃이 없고

꽃이 필 때는
잎이 진다

서로 그리워하며
만날 수 없는 사이

짝사랑이 좋아
이룰 수 없는 사랑.

Mutual Love Flower

Fresh
A noble flower
A pale yellow face

When the leaves come out
Without flowers

When flowers bloom
The leaves are lost

In a longing for each other
An unmeetable relationship

I like unrequited love
Love that can not be achieved.

살구꽃 피는 마을

제2부

아네모네꽃

산들바람으로
반짝이는 무늬를 들추어
나풀대는
봄바람 향기가 실려 왔다.

영춘화(迎春花)

간밤에 내린 비로
촉촉이

올망졸망
샛노란 눈망울
틔우고

봄나들이
노랑 미소

줄기마다
그림 그렸네!

Jasminum Nudiflorum

From the rain that last night
Moisturizing

In lots of small units
A yellow-eyed eye
In a bulge

Spring outing
A yellow smile

Per stem
I drew it!

아네모네꽃

이른 봄
주택가 여기저기에
화사한 목련화 꽃봉오리
우아하게 피어오르고

초야(草野) 곳곳에는
매화가 만발하여
벌 나비 윙윙거리네

고요한 골목길 정원에
핀
예쁘고 사랑스러운 아네모네꽃

산들바람으로
반짝이는 무늬를 들추어
나풀대는
봄바람 향기가 실려 왔다.

Anemone Flower

Early spring
All over the residential area
Bright magnolia bud
With graceful rise

There are many places in the field
In full bloom
Bee butterflies buzz

In the quiet alley garden
Flowering
A pretty, lovely anemone flower

In the breeze
With a glittering pattern
Fluttering
The scent of spring wind came in.

패랭이꽃

산간벽지(山間僻地)에서
잘 자라는 패랭이꽃은

열을 내리고
소변을 잘 보게 하며
혈압을 낮추는 데에
효과가 있고

잎, 줄기, 열매를 달여서
복용하면
대장염, 위염, 십이지장염 등에
효험이 있고

생리불순, 자궁염에도
효과가 있으며

씨앗은 한방에서
이뇨제로 쓰이네.

Pink Flowers

A secluded place in the mountain
The growing pink flower

With a fever
To pass the urine well
In the blood pressure lowering
It works

By afforesting leaves, stems, and berries
On dose
Colitis, gastritis, duodenitis etc.
Effective

I mean, menstrual irregularities, uterine infections
Effective

The seeds are in a herbal medicine shop
It's used as a diuretic.

갯버들꽃

따스한 햇볕이 봄으로 물들고
봄바람이 함초롬히 겨울을 털어낸 뒤
배시시 얼굴을 내민
갯버들 여린 싹

개울녘 할퀴고 간 꽃샘추위에
제 몸 낮춰
꿋꿋이 버틴
저 여린 꽃가지에
맺히는 꽃봉오리

달래 냉이 기지개 켤 때
허리를 곧추세워 외진 곳에

오롯이 소복하게
포근한 사랑으로
고개 드는 연둣빛 노란 꽃들.

Pussy Willow Flower

The warm sun is tinged with spring
The spring breezes have swept through the winter
A little face-out
Pussy willow buds

The cold of the flower spring
Lower your body!
A firm hold
On that little flower branch
Buds of flowers

Wild rocambole and shepherd's purse the stretching switch
In the remote place standing waist

Completely, abundantly
With warm love
The pale yellow flowers that look up.

매화가 만발할 때

겹겹이 둘러싸인
겨울의 껍질을 벗기고
따뜻한 봄의 기운을
알려주는 매화 봉오리

우아하면서도 화사한
동양의 여성스러운 꽃 매화
낯익은 모습 반갑고 눈물겹구나

은은한 향기 사방에 풍기며
세파에 시달린 우리를
마음의 고향으로 안내하는 매화

다시 봄이 오고
매화가 만발할 때
일 년 내내
그윽한 향기에 추억을 그린다.

When the Plum Blossoms

Layer‑enclosed
Peeling the winter
Warm spring weather
Informing plum bud

Graceful and bright
Feminine flower plums of the Orient
How nice and tearful to see you familiar

All over the soft scent
I'm not gonna let you
Plums to guide you to your home of mind

Spring is coming again
When the plum blossoms
All year round
I miss memories with a gentle scent.

철쭉꽃

이른 봄
깊은 산속
흐드러지게 핀
철쭉꽃
임 기다리네!

물소리, 새소리 들으며
군락을 이룬
청초하고 단아한 자태의
철쭉꽃
임 유혹하네!

순결하고 아름다운
철쭉꽃
임 사모하네!

사랑스러운 갖가지 색깔의
철쭉꽃 물결
임 추억 속으로 안내하네!

초여름
온 산야를 물들인
철쭉꽃
임 대초원으로 이끄네!

Royal Azalea Flower

Early spring
Deep mountain
Flowering splendidly
Royal azalea flower
Waiting for him!

Listening to the water, the birds
Community-shaped
Neat and simple
Royal azalea flower
Seduce him!

Pure and beautiful
Royal azalea flower
I adore you!

Lovely and colorful
Royal azalea flower wave
I'm leading you into memories!

Early summer
Being dyed all mountains
Royal azalea flower
Lead to the great prairie!

애쑥꽃

꽃샘추위 때
솜털 옷 걸치고
양지(陽地)마다 돋아나
봄의 향기를 알리는 애쑥

바구니에 칼자루를 쥐고
부드러울 때를 놓치지 않는 아낙네
언덕배기마다 털썩 주저앉아
꽃 그림을 그린다

여린 꽃이 피어 보지도 못한 체
예리한 칼끝으로 도려져
쌉싸래한 맛의 봄 향기 가득하네

쑥 개떡, 쑥 반찬, 쑥 국이 되어
보릿고개 넘기고

우리네 이웃
장수(長壽)도 하네!

Mugwort Flower

Due to the spring colds
In a fluffy suit
It springs up in every sunrise land
Mugwort to signal the scent of spring

With a knife in the basket
Aunt who doesn't miss the soft times
They are gonna sit down on every hillside
Draw a flower picture

I can't even see the flowers
Cut with a sharp tip of a knife
It's full of spring scents of a fresh taste

It becomes the rice cake, the side dish and the soup
Get over the period of spring poverty

Our neighbor
And a long life!

구절초꽃

그리움이 사무치는
하얀 구절초

산과 들
군락을 지어
수줍게 피어 있네!

청결하고 순결한 구절초
새싹 때 나물로 먹고
꽃과 가녀린 잎은
꽃 술떡, 연 명주, 꽃잎 차, 한약재
또는 베개를 만드니
향기 은은하네!

저무는 들녘에
더욱더 은은한 구절초

여기저기 저리도
저만치 피어 있네!

집 담장 아래
장독대 옆에
소박하고 청초하게
피어 있는 구절초

이 땅의 가을을
더욱 가을 하게 하네!

Dendranthema Flower

Longing
White dendranthema

Mountain fields
In a community
You're shy!

A clean and innocent dendranthema
And eat it as a herb
Flowers and thin leaves
The flower sake, lotus silk, petal tea, herbal medicine
Or make a pillow
Smells soft!

In the low fields
A more subtle dendranthema

All over the place
I'm a little bloomy!

Under the house fence
By the jangdokdae
Simple and neatly
Blossoming dendranthema

The autumn of this land
Let's make it fall even more!

씀바귀꽃

산과 들에
띄엄띄엄 노란 꽃송이

간밤 빗줄기에
털도 없이
줄기는 가늘며
위쪽에서 갈라진 네 모습

때 없이 찾아온 것은 아니지만
화들짝 놀라
미친 듯 뛰어다니는 바람이
꽃송이를 뒤흔들고

이른 봄 내내
목마름의 기다림
어린순을 식용으로

너를 뿌리째
약용으로
갖고 싶은 이 마음.

Lettuce Flower

In the mountains and fields
Sparsely yellow blossom

In the rain last night
Without tiny hair
The stem is thin
The splitting of your image from the top

I didn't come here without time
In a flash
A crazy wind
Rocking the flower buds

All early spring
A thirsty wait
For the edible soft bud

Rooted in you
For medicinal purposes
This heart I want.

도라지꽃

가냘픈 꽃
굵고 강인한 뿌리
옥색 치마로 여민

여인의 순결
하얀 도라지꽃

보랏빛으로
향기로움으로
영원한 사랑으로
미소 짓는 아낙네

눈에
선(禪)을 그리게 하네!

Bellflower

A thin flower
Thick and strong roots
Jade skirt

The virginity of a woman
White bellflower

In purple
Aromatically
With eternal love
A smiling woman

In the eye
Let him remember a Zen.

라일락 향기

살랑대는 바람결에
향긋한 향기로
가슴에 스미는 라일락

연보랏빛 꽃송이
코끝에 대고
살며시 눈 감으면

여린 빛의 꽃향기
숨 쉬는 대지마다
울려 퍼지고
설레는 가슴에
은은히 흘러

아득한
젊은 날의 봄날이
추억에 젖는 듯
라일락 향기에 숨어 오네!

Lilac Scent

In the wind
In a fragrant aroma
Lilac sink into my mind

A purple flower bud
On the tip of the nose
If you close your eyes gently

The scent of flowers of light
Every breathable earth
Resonating
In the throbbing chest
A subdued flow

Faraway
Springtime of a young day
As if it were a memory
Hiding in the scent of lilacs!

살구꽃 피는 마을

제3부

불두화의 미소

각박한 세상에도
선행과 보시로
푸른 원을 이루어 하나 되는 꽃

붓꽃 사랑

초여름에
살며시 고개 내밀어
미소 짓는 아이리스여

자주색 행운에
노란빛 기다림으로
바람이 살랑살랑
붓꽃을 흔들어

온종일
서로 기쁜 소식 전하는
신비한 붓꽃

자줏빛 향기로 꾸민 미소
영원한 사랑의 붓꽃!

Iris Love

Early summer
Give me your head gently
Smiling Iris

In purple luck
With a yellow wait
The wind is whispering
Shake the iris

All day
To share with delight each other
Mystical iris

A purple smile
The Iris of eternal love!

불두화의 미소

뭉글뭉글한 꽃잎으로
처음 필 때는 연초록색
만개했을 때는 눈부신 하얀색
시들 때는 빛바랜 연보랏빛

고깔을 쓴
세 갈래 잎 모양
열매도 없는 승무화(僧舞花) 군락

꽃잎마다 하늘이 열리고
뭉게구름이 흘러
바람에 흩날리는 꽃비

각박한 세상에도
선행과 보시로
푸른 원을 이루어 하나 되는 꽃

사찰마다 꽃등을 다는 사월 초파일
꽃송이마다 부처를 그리는 듯
하얀 꽃이 미소 짓듯 앞다투어 핀다.

A Smile of Guelder Rose

With a soft petal
Green in the first period
A dazzling white when full bloom
Faded violet light when it was withering

In a cone
Three-pronged leaf shape
Fruitless sublime community

The sky opens for each petal
A cloud of lumps flows
A wind-scattered rain

In a world of hardship
Good deeds and alms
Flowers in a blue circle

April 8th Yeondeunghoe with flowers for each temple
Like a flowering Buddha
White flowers smile.

산수국꽃

남빛 나비
에워싸
꽃으로 피었다

그 꽃 안으로
꽃봉오리 내려앉아
수많은 수국꽃 빚어내니

지나가는 나그네
긴 호흡으로
갈 길을 서둘지 않고

카메라를 손끝으로 눌러
가벼운 떨림 속
찰칵!

자주색 나비가
꽃으로 형상화한
저 은은한 날갯짓

스며 나오는 네 모습!

Hydrangea Flower

Navy blue butterfly
Encircle
Bloom with flowers

In the flower
Sit down the buds
I've made a lot of hydrangea

A passing passerby
Long-breathingly
Without rushing to the road

Press the camera with your fingertips
Light tremor
With a snap!

Purple butterfly
Flower-shaped
That subtle wings

Your permeation!

해바라기꽃

만인을 위해 서 있는
외로운 해바라기
비바람 태풍과 맞서며

긴 고개를 햇빛 따라
사방으로 휘청거리며
우리에게 미소를 던져 주네

노란 얼굴에 까만 눈동자
앞을 향해 꽃눈을 틔우며

끊임없이 타오르는 주홍빛 얼굴
그 뜨거운 사랑
그 눈빛
저 태양의 꽃이여!

Sunflower

Standing for all
Lonely sunflower
Against the storms and rains

Along the long head in the sunlight
Stumbled all over
They're giving us a smile

A yellow face, black eyes
With a flower eye in front of him

A constantly burning scarlet face
The hot love
The eyes
That flower of the sun!

나팔꽃

어둠이 지나
아침이슬 머금고
담벼락에 기대서서
가냘픈 손을 저어
어디로 가는가?

네 고운 꽃잎으로
그리움의 나팔 소리 들리는 듯
보랏빛 자태로 아침 햇살 부른다

한낮의 햇볕 따라
고운 꽃잎 접어
푸름으로 솟아오르네

밤하늘의 별을 그리며
수많은 사연 쌓아
다시 아침을 맞는다.

Morning Glory

Past the darkness
Morning dew
Lean against the wall
Shake a soft hand
Where are we going?

With your fine petals
As if I could hear the trumpet of longing
The morning sun is sung in a purple figure

In the sun of the day
Fold the fine petals
It rises in blue

Star-picking in the night sky
A great deal of stories
It's breakfast again.

호박꽃

이른 아침
밤이슬 가득 머금고
그윽한 향기 품으며
미명을 밝히는
샛노란 모습의 호박꽃 물결
호박잎 바다

벌 나비 떼 분주히 날고
무더운 여름 한나절
짙푸른 호박잎 그늘에서
우아한 나팔소리 그친다

삶으로 가득 찬 호박꽃
애호박이 주렁주렁
맷돌 호박 둥실둥실

호박전에
호박죽
많이 먹을수록
생기발랄하고

두고두고 부르는 그대 이름
아름다운 호박꽃!

Pumpkin Flower

Early morning
With a full night dew
With a breathtaking scent
Illustrating the beauty of the world
Amber flower waves of a bright yellow
Pumpkin leaf sea

A bunch of bees and butterfly flying around
A hot summer day
In the shade of the dark blue pumpkin leaf
The graceful trumpet stops

Amber flowers filled with life
Amber-snatched
Millstone pumpkin floating light

Before pumpkin
Pumpkin porridge
The more you eat
Lively

Your name you call
Beautiful pumpkin flower!

밤꽃 사랑

산간벽지 어디서나
손길이 닿지 않는 그곳에

밤 숲에서 불어오는
농밀한 밤꽃 향기
들이쉬며

아이보리 꽃들이
생명을 불살라

싱그러운 초록 분신
방울방울 맺는다

제 몸 가누지 못해
수줍게 영글어진 그 자태

치마에 가득 담으니
세상을 다 가진 듯
가슴 벅차오른다.

Chestnut Flower Love

Wherever the secluded place in mountains
Where you can't reach

In a chestnut tree-forest
A dense scent of chestnut flowers
Inhaling

Ivory flowers
Burn your life

A fresh green alter ego
Bear a bell

I can't keep my body up
The shyly gleaming figure

I'm gonna be in my skirt
As if he had the whole world
My heart is surging.

살구꽃 피는 마을

봄바람 살랑살랑
동구 밖 개울가에
외로이 서 있는 살구나무
한그루

진분홍 색깔로
발그무레하게 피워내
오가는 행인
걸음을 멈추네

살구나무 가지마다
밤낮으로 아름답게
그리움을 터트리다가

세찬 비바람에
우수수 떨어지는 꽃바람으로

까마득한 지난날이
개울물과 졸졸 졸
스쳐 흘러가네!

Apricot-Flowered Village

Spring breeze salang
In the stream outside the village
Apricot tree standing alone
A single

In pink
Blooming with pink color
A passing passerby
Stop walking

Per apricot branch
Day and night beautifully
I miss it

In the wind and rain
To the flower wind falling at one time

A long time ago
Murmurous stream water
It's going by!

아카시아꽃

싱그러운 오월

봄바람 속에서
하얀 꽃잎은
눈처럼 흩날리고
또 쌓여
오뉴월 한나절의 적막을 깨고

말없이
가슴으로 이야기하는
아카시아 꽃향기

그리운 그대에게
발걸음을 멈추게 하네!

Acacia Flower

Fresh May

In the spring breeze
White petals
Scattering like snow
And then piled up
Breaking the desolation of early summer

In silence
Heart-to-heart
Acacia flower scent

To miss you
It's stopping!

들국화 향기

들국화 꽃잎에
영롱한 아침이슬

남쪽 산야(山野)에서
임이 찾아오니
들국화 향기
바람 타고 흐르네

저 창천(蒼天)을 바라보라
삶이 순간임을 몰라
헤매던 야조(野鳥)들이
가까이 날고

온 세상 미물(微物)들이
반겨 다가오니

산천(山川)이 의의(意義)가 되고
삶은 역동(力動)하네

아(峨)!
하늘의 길이 열리고
들국화 향기 진동하니
강산이 다시 푸르러라.

The Scent of Wild Chrysanthemum

In the wild chrysanthemum petal
A brilliant morning dew

In the southern mountains
You come to see me
The scent of wild chrysanthemum
It's in the wind

Look at that blue heavens
I don't know life is a moment
The wildfowls
Fly nearly

The world's trifles
I'm glad to see you

It is meaningful to be born in the mountains
Life is dynamic

Ah!
The path of the sky opens
The aroma of wild chrysanthemums
The river is blue again.

복사꽃 피는 언덕

봄비가 내린 후
아지랑이 하늘거리는 봄날

바위틈에
진달래 피고
개나리 샛노랗다

감미로운 향기를 품은 매화
빛깔이 고운 이화
멀리 있어도 눈에 잘 보이고

화사한 벚꽃과 살구꽃
엷은 분홍빛 복사꽃
활짝 피어
바람에 미소 짓네!

밤나무 감나무…

언덕으로 달리는 봄
향기를 가득 담은 꽃의 바다에
잠시 머문다

Peach-Flowered Hill

After the spring rain
A hazy spring day

In the rocky crevice
Azalea is in bloom
Be a forsythia yellow

Plums with a sweet scent
A fine-colored pear flower
I can see it in the distance

Bright cherry blossoms and apricot flowers
Pale pink radiant flower
Burst into bloom broad
Smiling in the wind!

Chestnut tree, persimmon tree…

Spring running into the hill
In the sea of the flower full of the aroma
Stay a while.

할미꽃과 함께

어린 시절

이른 봄
뒷동산에 올라
무덤가에 핀
정겨운 할미꽃
신비한 듯 바라본다

풀 향보다 은은하게
봄소식을 전해주는 할미꽃
우리 마음속에
고개 숙여
끈질김과 강인함을 일깨워 주고
소박한 정서를 불러일으켜
옛 생각에 젖게 한다

슬픈 전설을 간직한
사랑의 할미꽃
누군가를 그리워하는
내 가슴 한구석에
추억으로
늘 피어 있으리.

With the Pasqueflower

Childhood

Early spring
I'm on the back hill
Bloom by the grave
A sweet pasqueflower
Look at it mysteriously

Subtly more than grass
Pasqueflower which delivers the spring news
In our hearts
Bow your head
Reminding you of your tenacity and strength
Evokes a simple emotion
Make one's old thoughts wet

A sad legend
A flower of love
A missive person
In the corner of my chest
In memory
Pasqueflower always bloom.

살구꽃 피는 마을

제4부

코스모스 연가

한 허리 한 움큼
하늘거리는 고운 물결
따스한 햇볕 스미는 영혼

명자꽃

봄이면
아련히 떠오르는 명자꽃

움츠렸던 대지에
촉촉이 비 내리면
대자연이 부르는
생명의 부활, 명자꽃

봄날의 빨간 설렘처럼

시샘을 하는지
사이가 좋은지
옹기종기 모여서
매혹적인 웃음 듬뿍 짓네!

집 담장 밖
거리의 울타리
어디에서나 볼 수 있는
아가씨 나무, 명자화 님

무어라
애기할 듯
망설이는 듯
얼굴 불그스레

나에게 사랑을
고백하려나 봐!

Lagenaria Flower

In spring
A faintly rising lagenaria

On a shrunken site
When the moist rains
The great nature
Resurrection of Life, the Flower of the Master

Like the red throbbing of spring

If you're jealous
Is it good to know
In a huddle
You're making me laugh so fascinating!

Outside the house fence
A street fence
Ubiquitous
Lady Tree, Myongjahwa

Anything!
As if to say
As if he was hesitant
Face reddish

Love for me
He's going to confess!

눈부신 벚꽃

봄은 바야흐로 태생지
남녘 제주도 한라산 기슭에서
막 핀 산벚꽃과 함께 시작하네

활짝 핀 벚꽃 하얗게 흩날리어
지르밟고 지나가는 군상들을
뒤돌아보지 않고
그리운 봄을 숨어서
앞서가듯 북상한다

빛나는 봄날
화사한 벚꽃 활짝
봄나들이 북적거려
삼천리 금수강산에
순백의 향연을 펼친다

온 세상에 활짝 핀
새하얀 눈꽃
순수함으로 피어난
그 황홀한 고요

만물이 소생하는 봄
눈부신 벚꽃의 유혹에
겨우내 움츠렸던 어깨를 편다.

A Dazzling Cherry Blossom

Spring is born at the height
At the foot of Mt. Halla in the south Jeju Island
It's just starting with the flowering mountain cherry blossoms

A wide-open cherry blossom white
I'm gonna have to get a bunch of
Without looking back
I'm hiding the nostalgic spring
Head north ahead

A brilliant spring day
A bright cherry blossom
The spring outing is crowded
In the beautiful land of Korea.
Spread a feast of pure white

All over the world
White snowflake
Purely-bred
The ecstatic silence

Spring when all things are resuscitated
I'm not sure I'm going to be able to
I open my shrugged shoulders.

민들레꽃

칙칙한 땅거죽에서 돋아나는
연초록빛의 샛노란 민들레
화창한 하늘에
지저귀는 새소리 들으며
숲속 바람 타고
봄을 알리네!

산마루에 아지랑이 아물아물
들판엔 짙어 오는 신록
침묵 속에 팽창하는
대지의 가슴에
가녀린 미소로 피어난
환한 민들레 꽃송이

나비가 사뿐사뿐
꿀벌이 윙윙
뭇시선이 머무는 곳에
촉촉해진 눈망울로

햇살 가득한 나날
바람 따라
또 어디론가 훌쩍 떠난다.

Dandelion Flower

A squishy earthen porridge
A pale green yellow dandelion
In the sunny sky
With a chirping bird
In the wind of the forest
Let's see spring!

A haze-healing on the ridge
A thick green in the fields
Dilatating in silence
In the heart of the earth
A thin smile
Bright dandelion blossom

The butterflies are fluttering
Bee buzz
Where the eyes stays
Moistened eyelid

Day after day full of sunshine
By the wind
He leaves somewhere else.

장미꽃

그대
눈감아도 느낄 것 같은
미려한 얼굴 떠올리며
싱싱한 생명력
몽실몽실
요염한 자태로 미소 짓고

너를 바라보다
품고 싶었던
상큼한 순결
정열적인 사랑

너를 꼬여 내고자
매일 되새긴
그 현란한 빛깔
도발적인 향기에
하늘이 어질어질

내 뜨거운 숨소리를
녹슨 심장도
피를 용솟음치게 하는
가시에 엮으며
장미 한 다발을 그린다

언제나 그 자리
꺾일까 봐 목숨 내걸고
연인보다 더욱
매혹적인 몸부림으로
당신을 매료시키는
그 이름 장미꽃.

Rose Flower

You are
Like you're gonna feel
With a beautiful face
Fresh vitality
Plumply
With a smile in a sly manner

Look at you
I wanted to have
Fresh purity
Passionate love

I'm going to have to twist you
Daily-recalling
The dazzling color
In a provocative scent
The sky is dizzy

I'm gonna have to hear my hot breath
Rusty heart chart
Blood-raising
Woven into thorns
Draw a bunch of roses

Always there
I'm afraid I'll break it
More than a lover
With a fascinating struggle
That fascinated you
The name rose.

목련화(木蓮花)

지난 긴 겨울
봄바람에
희고 우아한 모습으로
벙글벙글
환하게 다가와
내 마음 온통 설렘으로 가득하네!

구름송이 피는 언덕에서
네 화사한 가슴
카메라에 담으며
순결한 미소 꼬여 낸다

한순간
간곡히 일러둔 사랑
또다시
아쉬움만 남기고
떠나 버리는 지순(至純)한 목련화.

Magnolia Blossom

The last long winter
In the spring breeze
In a white and elegant manner
Smilingly
Come brightly
My whole heart is full of excitement!

In the cloudy hills
Your bright heart
In camera
Twist a pure smile

For a moment
A love of love
Again
With a pity
A serious magnolia that leaves.

산수유화(山茱萸花)

산수유
아직은 이른 봄
눈발 맞는 꽃봉오리

메마른 가지 위에
새 세상 열려 오는가!

개울가
저 산야에
봄이 오는 소리

석조(石棗) 홍옥(紅玉) 그리는
바쁜 마음에
노란 네 잎의 꽃을 피운다.

Cornelian Flower

Cornelian
Early spring
Snow-flake bud

On a dry branch
Come to the new world!

A stream
In that mountain
The sound of spring

Stone, red-ruby
In a busy heart
Flowers of four yellow leaves.

코스모스 연가

애처로운 미소
가냘픈 몸짓
가녀린 여인의 향기

한 허리 한 움큼
하늘거리는 고운 물결
따스한 햇볕 스미는 영혼

누구를 기다리나
청초한 너의 모습

친구와 벗하여
옛 임을 못 견디게 그리며
오늘도
바람결에 쓸쓸히 흔들리누나.

Cosmos Love Song

A pathetic smile
A gentle gesture
The scent of a slender woman

A handful of waists
A fine wave of the sway
A warm sun-smeared soul

Who are you waiting for?
A neat figure of you

With a friend
In longing for old friend unbearably
Today
You're so lonely in the wind.

찔레꽃

우리네 길가에
정갈하게 피는 찔레꽃
바위틈 척박한 땅
마다치 않고 뿌리내리는
흙 내음 간직한 꽃

초록이 흐르는 계절에
그리운 가슴 가만히 열어
외로운 소녀의 넋으로
먼 여행에서 돌아와
송이송이 하얗게 웃으며

내 사랑 깊이
찔레 향으로 여름 알리고
무상(無常)한 사랑으로 서 있네

여린 순은 허기 달래고
고적감(孤寂感)도 다독여주는
시골 찔레꽃

더욱더 그리워라
찔레꽃 피는 그 길
숨은 듯 반가운 찔레꽃이여!

Multiflora

On our side of the road
A neatly blooming prickly flower
A rocky land
Unwillingly rooted
A flower with a soil

In the green season
Open your nostalgic heart
With the soul of a lonely girl
I'm back from a long trip
With a white smile

My love depth
I'll let you know the summer with a flavour
Standing with free love

A soft bud soothes hunger
It pats to the loneliness sensitivity
A country multiflora

Miss you more and more
The way the prickly flowers bloom
Hidden, nice muliflora!

억새꽃

은빛 물결이 투명하게
흐르는 가을 속으로
모진 세월을 스친 억새꽃

풀벌레 소리 들으며
외로움을 느낄 때

못다 한 꿈
시린 가슴에 담아 놓고
속삭이는 실바람에
아픔을 보듬고

가을 달빛 그리워
나부끼는 억새의 춤사위에
파란 하늘 우러러
가을 속으로 물들어 간다.

Miscanthus

Silvery waves are transparent
Into the flowing autumn
A flower of the cherished age

With the sound of grassworms
When I feel lonely

A dream of misery
In a bitter heart
In a whisper of wind
With pain

I miss the autumn moonlight
At the dance moves of fluttering miscanthus
Up to the blue sky
It is stained into the autumn.

웃음꽃

3살쯤의 사내아이가
외발자전거를
타고 가다가

차가 다니는
위험한 골목길에서

갑자기
멈칫하며

마주 오는 어른한테
순간
순수하게 활짝
미소 지으며

"안녕하세요!"

그때
지은 미소는
나에게 던져진
최고의 감탄사!

A Laughing Flower

A boy about three years old
I'm gonna need a single-footed bike
On the ride

Car-riding
In a dangerous alley

Suddenly
With a pause

I'm gonna tell the grown-up
Moment
Purely wide
Smilingly

Hi!

Then
The smile you made
Thrown at me
The best exclamation!

살구꽃 피는 마을

제5부

눈새기꽃

엄동설한 숨죽였던 생명
하얀 그리움에 수줍은 듯
시린 가슴 달래며
얼굴 내민 샛노란 얼음새꽃

에델바이스꽃

천상의 향기로
설원에서 태어나

이루지 못한 사랑
아쉬워하며

녹색의 세상에
청아하게 피었네

기다리는 사랑
운명처럼 사라지고

단절된 그리움에
날개 달고

사랑을 얻고자
고난을 극복한다.

Edelweiss Flower

In the heavenly scent
Born in snowy fields

Unfulfilled love
With regret

In a world of green
Bloom purely

Waiting love
Disappearing like fate

In the lost longing
With wings

To gain love
The hardship is overcome.

설중 매화

차디찬 겨울
누구나 견디기 어려운
엄동설한 삭풍에
빛나는 너의 영혼
눈 속에 꽃 피워 온
그 고결한 성품

하늬바람에 흔들림 없이
백야의 신비를 품으며
세상 향해 피는 설중매
잔설이 남아있는 산자락에
봄기운이 찾아들어
제일 먼저 터트리는
저 강인한 몸짓

따사로운 햇볕에 눈 녹은 물이
꽃잎을 촉촉이 적시며
반짝반짝 빛나는 설중 매화

꽃들의 제왕인가!
눈 속에 핀 매화의 꽃망울들이
우리의 가슴속을
시리도록 헤집으며
참으로 아름답게 손짓하네!

Plum Blossoming in the Snow

A cold winter
Hard for anyone to bear
In the sharp wind
Your shining soul
Flowering in the snow
The noble character

Without shaking in the wind
With the mystery of nights with the midnight sun
Plum blossom in the face of the world
In the mountain where the snow remains
Spring energy is in the air
First thing I want
That tough gesture

The warm sun is making snow melt
The moisturizing wets petal
A sparkling snowy plum

Lord of the Flowers!
The flowering buds of plum blossoming in the snow
We're going to have to the chest
In a shimmering manner
How beautifully beckoning!

동백꽃

긴 긴 매서운 겨울 지나며

붉고 시린 눈물을 지닌
남해의 겨울 동백꽃이
청청하고 싱그러운 생명력을
토해내듯 붉디붉게 피어나네!

청춘이 아쉬운 듯
그윽한 향기와 고결한 자태로
온 산과 바다에 영혼을 흩뿌리고
온종일 정열을 불사르네!

세월은 흘러
벌, 나비, 새들은
추억으로 사라지고

몰골 흉한 꽃송이
하소연 한마디 못하고
대지의 품으로 곤두박질
최후를 맞는 꽃들의 널브러짐

전설을 아련히 가슴에 묻고
다소곳이 엎어져
바람이 스쳐 지나가네!

Camellia Flower

A long, bitter winter

With red and bitter tears
The winter camellia of the South Sea
Clean, fresh vitality
It's blooming red as if it's vomiting!

Youth is a pity
With a gentle scent and a noble figure
Spreading souls all over the mountains and the sea
You've been burning your passion all day!

The years pass
Bees, butterflies, birds
Disappear into memories

A wild flower bud
Without a word of complaint
Plummeting into the arms of the earth
The sprawling of the last flowers

With a legend in his heart
A little overturned
The wind is coming through!

메꽃

산간벽지 논밭 둑에
구불구불 틀고 앉아
산들바람 맞으며
피는 메꽃

고향 들판에서 수줍은 듯
연분홍빛 꽃으로 나를 반기네

둑 밑에 흙이 떨어져
보이는 하얀 메 뿌리
세상 티끌 씻겨
한결 맑아진 듯

그냥 바지에 문대어
질 건 씹어도
얼굴 붉힐 일 없는
메꽃은

어린 시절
아련하게
떠오르는 추억의 꽃.

Convolvulus

On the bank of a field
Slide in a twist
In the breeze
A blooming convolvulus

Shy in the field of home
You welcome me with pink flowers

The soil falls under the bank
Visible white convolvulus root
Wash the world's dust
As if it were clearer

Just put your trousers on
Jingle even if chewed
Blushless your face
Convolvulus

Childhood
Dimly
Flowers of memories that come to mind.

눈새기꽃

겨우내 다진 그리움으로
솟아오른 진한 생명의 혼
봄눈으로 품어 녹이고

그 위를
이른 봄바람이 스친다

엄동설한 숨죽였던 생명
하얀 그리움에 수줍은 듯
시린 가슴 달래며
얼굴 내민 샛노란 얼음새꽃

찬바람이 떠나기 전
뭇 봄꽃들의 개화를 이끌려
노란 눈꽃으로
이정표를 세우네!

Adonis Flower

With a longing for the last winter
The soul of a rising, deep life
Melt with spring snow

On top of it
The early spring breezes brush

A life of a prudent breath
Shy with white nostalgia
Sootheing the heart
A bright yellow adonis flower

Before the cold wind
The flowering of the spring flowers is led
Yellow‐eyed
You're setting a milestone!

달맞이꽃

밝고 야한 달빛 아래
달맞이꽃 무리
수줍은 듯

길가에
그리움을 가득 채워
밤이 이슥토록
자신의 향기를 터트리네

노란 그리움으로 피는 그 꽃
풀벌레 울음소리
귓가를 스칠 때

우리의 기다림도
달이 뜨고 별이 지는
그런 밤에 있으리.

Evening Primrose

Under the bright, jaunty moonlight
A Evening Primrose herd
Shyly

By the road
Fill your longing
The night is so great
He bursts his scent

The flowers that bloom with yellow nostalgia
A grassworm cry
When it brushes my ears

Our waiting
The moon rises and stars fall
I'll be there that night.

칡꽃

태곳적부터 이어온
인류의 이해관계처럼
계곡마다 지천으로 얽혀 자라는
무수한 칡덩굴

적막함에 무엇엔가 홀린 듯
무모한 줄 모르고
허공을 향해
사력을 다해 기어오른다

산골짜기 시원한 바람
벽산(碧山)에 짙은 남보랏빛 향기로
곱게 물든 칡꽃이

살랑이는 모습으로
닿을 듯
내게 다가온다.

Kudzu Flower

From the beginning
Like the interests of mankind
Every valley is a river-growing
Myriad vines

In the silence of something
Without knowing it was reckless
Toward the air
Climb with all your might

A cool breeze in the valley
With a deep, south purple scent on the mountain
A finely dyed kudzu flower

With a gentle look
Adjoiningly
He comes to me.

겨울꽃

그 길 위에 서 있는
풀과 나무 잠든 절기

천년만년
밤에 내린 눈꽃과 비조차
수빙(樹氷)으로
눈꽃 피운 나목들

군데군데 바위틈
나뭇가지 끝
계곡 물길에

눈보라 흩날리며
겨울꽃을 빚는다.

Winter Flower

Standing on the road
A grass and tree-sleeping season

Myriad years
Snow flower and rain that fell at night
By glazing ice on trees
Snowflakes of the trees

A rocky gap
Branch tip
In the valley

In a blizzard
Make winter flowers.

해당화 사랑

은빛 모래밭
파란 파도 소리에
내 마음 적셔놓고
고운 자태 뽐내며
쪽빛 하늘 그리는구나

갈매기 울음소리에
한 송이 꽃을 피우고
아지랑이 여울 춤에
그리움 담아

낙조처럼 멀어져 간
새색시 손짓에
붉게 물들인 해당화

시나브로 초록빛으로
바닷가 저 멀리
갯바람 불어와
모래알이 반짝반짝

임 오실 길목마다
향기로운 홍자색 꽃등으로
속절없이 피고 지네!

Sweetbrier Love

Silver sand
The sound of blue waves
I'm soaking up my mind
In a fine manner
You draw a indigo sky

In the gull's cries
With a flower
The haze and dance of the rapids
With longing

A fall away
In a new bride gesture
Reddish-colored sweetbrier

With green color gradually
Far by the sea
A sea breeze blow
Sandy gleams

Every road to come
With the fragrant reddish-red flower lamp
Blooming and wither hopelessly!

풍접초꽃

꽃잎이 나비 날개를 연상케 하여
나비가 바람에 날아가는 형상
풍접초화(風蝶草花)

고향은 머나먼 중앙아메리카
우리나라 기후에 적응하여
귀화에 성공한 꽃

가을에 떨어진 씨가
추운 겨울을 이기고서
봄이면 싹을 틔우고
여름이면 화사한 꽃들을 피움에

바람에 한들한들
꽃으로 날아든 나비들을
연상케 하는 아름다운 풍접초꽃은

가지 끝에 둥글게 모여 피는
꽃 뭉치의 모양이
왕관과 비슷하여 왕관꽃

결혼할 때
쓰는 족두리와 비슷하여 족두리꽃

꽃말은 질투와 불안정!

Windy Butterfly Flower

Petals remind me of butterfly wings
A butterfly flying in the wind
Windy butterfly flower

Central America, far away from home
In the climate of our country
A flower that has succeeded in naturalization

A fall-falling seed
After a cold winter
In spring, they sprout
In the summer, you'll have to make a flower

The wind is shaking
The butterflies that fly in flowers
The beautiful, Windy butterfly flowers of the association

A rounded bloom at the end of a branch
The shape of the flower bundle
A crown-like flower

When you're married
The headpiece flower it is similar to the headpiece used

Flower words are jealousy, instability!

겨울 진달래꽃

가는 겨울이 아쉬운 듯
이른 봄이
진달래 꽃망울을
온 산야에 흩어 뿌린다

겨우내 기다리던
봄날의 분홍 꿈 그리며
하늘거리는 아지랑이 속에
그리움이
조심조심 부풀어 오른다

여기저기
찾아오는 갖가지 봄의 향연이
살며시 고개 들어
웃음 짓는다

가까이 보면
더욱 그리운
연분홍빛 아픔
활활 타올라
사랑의 열병 앓는다

봄이 무르익으며
고운 빛깔의 겨울 진달래
봄바람에 흐느끼듯 떨고 있네!

Winter Azalea Flower

The winter is a pity
Early spring
Azalea flower
Spread all over the mountains

I've been waiting
In the pink dream of spring
In the haze of the sky
Nostalgia
It swells carefully

Here and there
The feast of spring
Gently lift your head
He laughs

At close range
More missed
A pale pink pain
A lively burn
I have a fever of love

Spring ripens
Winter azaleas in fine color
I'm shivering in the spring breeze!

살구꽃 피는 마을

초판인쇄 2020년 8월 25일 초판발행 2020년 8월 30일

지은이   장현경
펴낸이   장현경 펴낸곳   엘리트출판사
등록일   2013년 2월 22일 제2013-10호

서울특별시 광진구 긴고랑로15길 11 (중곡동)
전화 010-5338-7925
E-mail : wedgus@hanmail.net

정가 11,000원

ISBN 979-11-87573-23-4 03810